The Duck in the Hole

by Mary Vigliante Szydlowski

illustrated by Lori Kiplinger Pandy

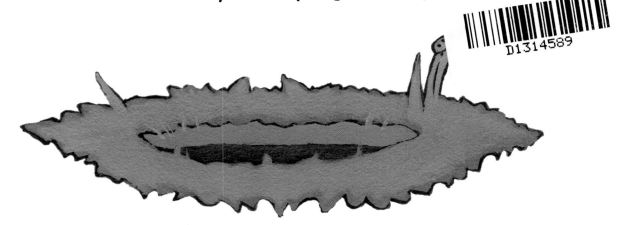

The Duck in the Hole
By
Mary Vigliante Szydlowski
Illustrated by Lori Kiplinger Pandy

Text Copyright © 2007 Mary Vigliante Szydlowski
Book design and illustrations © 2007 Lori Kiplinger Pandy

Published by
Operation Outreach–USA Press
Holliston, Massachusetts

ISBN 978-0-9792144-1-7

Printed in the United States of America

For Frank and Carrie with love.

Keesha heard a quack.
She looked around the yard.

"Quack."

The sound was coming from
a hole in the ground.

Keesha ran to the hole and looked in.

She was surprised to find a little brown duck at the bottom.

"Quack, quack," it cried.

The duck looked scared. The hole was narrow and deep. The little duck couldn't jump or fly out.

"You poor thing. How did you get down there?" Keesha asked. "Don't worry. I'll get you out."

Keesha got down on her hands and knees. She reached into the hole, but couldn't get the duck. Her arms were too short.

"Quack, quack," the little duck cried again.

She thought about putting a rope down the hole. Then she remembered that ducks had wings, not hands. They couldn't climb ropes!

What if she tied a basket to the end of the rope?

The duck could jump into the basket and Keesha could pull it out. Keesha looked at the hole. No, that wouldn't work. The hole wasn't big enough. There wasn't room in there for both the duck and a basket.

Maybe she could get a shovel and make the hole bigger. Dig it out a little.

No, she'd better not. No matter how careful she was, rocks and dirt could fall into the hole.

They might hit the duck and hurt it.

The machine they used to clean the rugs had a big long hose. Maybe Keesha could use it to suck the duck out of the hole.

No, that was a bad idea. It might pull the duck's feathers out.

Then it couldn't fly.

What should she do????

Her mother and father would know what to do. Keesha was going to look for them when she saw the neighbor's cat. It had heard the quacking too. It was walking toward the hole.

"Go home, Tiger," Keesha yelled.

"Woof, woof."
Keesha turned to look. Red, the dog from up the street, was running toward her. "Oh, no," Keesha said. "Not you too?"

Red ran to the hole and looked in.

He wagged his tail and barked.

"Quack! Quack! Quack!!!"

the duck cried in fear.

Keesha jumped up and down and waved her arms around.

"Get out of here," she yelled.

The dog ran out of the yard. So did the cat. But they didn't go far. They sat on the sidewalk and watched Keesha.

Keesha thought....

and thought...

and thought
some more.

Then she got an idea.

A great idea!

Keesha ran to get the garden hose. It was on the ground by the side of the house. She pulled it across the yard to the hole and turned it on.

The hole began to fill with water.

The duck quacked and splashed as the water rose higher and higher.

The little duck soon floated to the top.

"See, I told you I'd get you out," Keesha said.

The duck looked up at her. "Quack."

"You're welcome," she laughed.

Keesha smiled and waved as she watched the duck spread its wings and fly away.

"Good-bye little duck," she called.

She couldn't wait to tell her mom
and dad about the duck in the hole
and how she'd set it free.

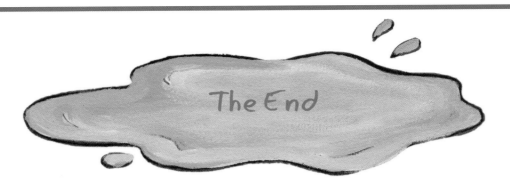

The End

About Operation Outreach—USA

Operation Outreach—USA (OO—USA) provides free literacy and character education programs to elementary and middle schools across the country.

Because reading is the gateway to success, leveling the learning field for at—risk children is critical. By giving books to students to own, confidence is built and motivated readers are created. OO—USA selects books with messages that teach compassion, respect and determination. OO—USA involves the school and the home with tools for teachers and parents to nurture and guide children as they learn and grow.

More than one million children in schools in all fifty states have participated in the program thanks to the support of a broad alliance of corporate, foundation and individual sponsors.

To learn more about Operation Outreach—USA and how to help, visit www.oousa.org, call 1-800-243-7929, or email jgolden@oousa.org.

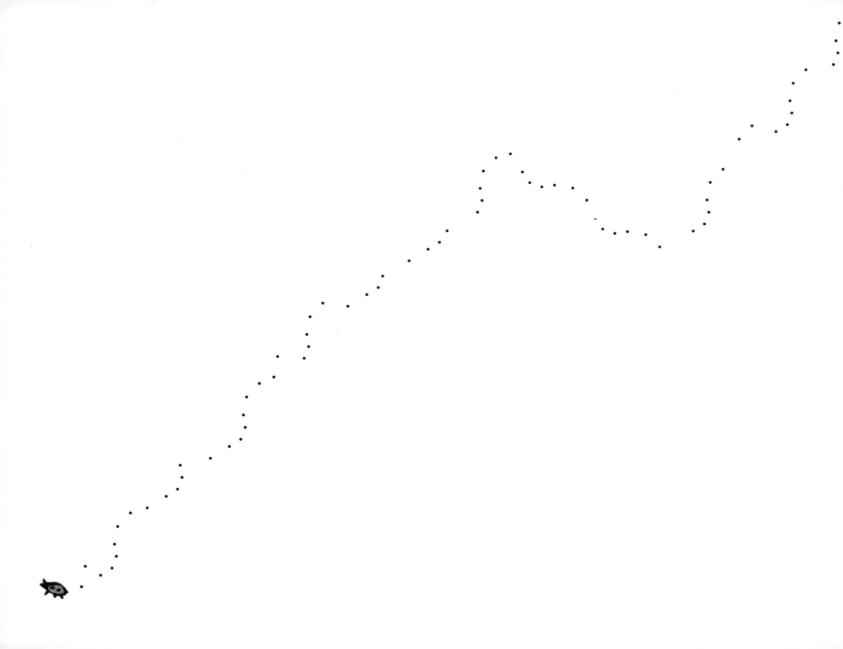

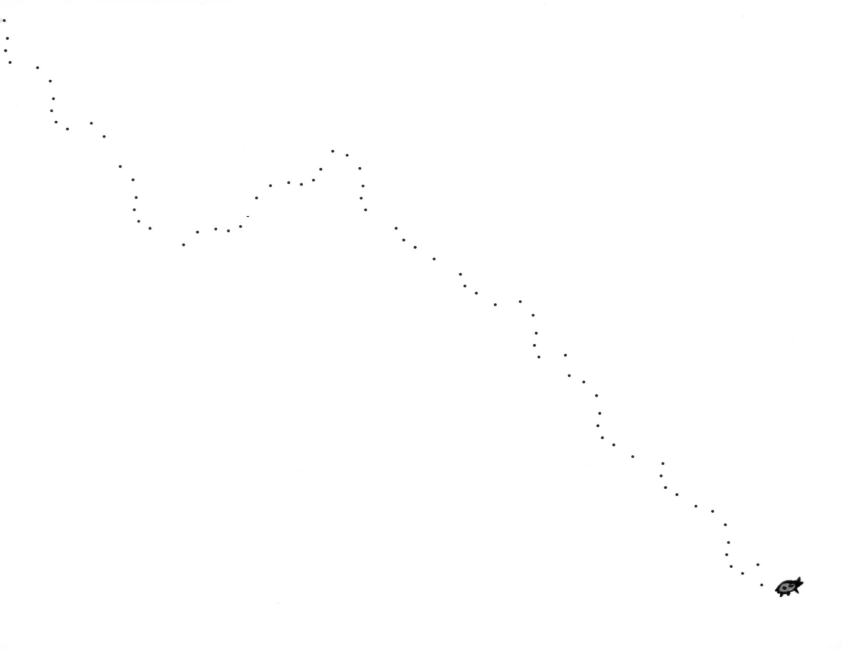